SISTER YESSA'S STORY

by **KAREN GREENFIELD** ◆ illustrated by **CLAIRE EWART**

A Laura Geringer Book

An Imprint of HarperCollins*Publishers*

SISTER YESSA'S STORY
Text copyright © 1992 by Karen Radler Greenfield
Illustrations copyright © 1992 by Claire Ewart
Printed in the U.S.A. All rights reserved.
Typography by Anahid Hamparian
1   2   3   4   5   6   7   8   9   10
First Edition

Library of Congress Cataloging-in-Publication Data
Greenfield, Karen.
   Sister Yessa's story / by Karen Greenfield ;
illustrated by Claire Ewart.
        p.   cm.
   "A Laura Geringer book."
   Summary: Dark clouds gather as Yessa walks to her
brother's place, telling a story as she goes about the
early days of the earth; and the animals follow her
two by two to listen.
   ISBN 0-06-020278-5. — ISBN 0-06-020279-3 (lib. bdg.)
   [1. Animals—Fiction.   2. Creation—Fiction.
3. Noah's ark—Fiction.] I. Ewart, Claire, ill.   II. Title.
PZ7.G8453Si   1992   91-15634
[E]—dc20   CIP
                                                     AC

For Caitlin and Nicholas
—K.G.

For Grandpa Curtis on his 100th,
and in memory of Grandma,
who lovingly shared seventy of
those years with him
—C.E.

Big, gray clouds were gathering in the distance. Yessa, the storyteller, wanted to be at her brother's place before the rain. It was going to be a long, long walk, but a story would make it go faster. Yessa cupped her hands together and called as loudly as she could, "Would anyone like to hear a story?" She called to the north, to the south, to the east, and to the west.

Two goldfinches flying overhead dipped closer to hear Yessa's story. Two mountain lions turned to follow Yessa as she walked to her brother's house. Two jackrabbits joined the others, and so did two bighorn sheep, two quail, and two armadillos. Two snakes slithered around, and two small mice found a safe place to listen. Then Yessa began her story.

"Once upon a time," said Yessa, "when the world was very new, a Great Turtle walked the earth, carrying all the animals of the world on his back. As he walked, the Great Turtle grew tired. 'If only some of the animals would get off my back,' he thought, 'perhaps I could lie down and rest for a while.'

But the Great Turtle loved all the animals and did not want to part with any of them. So round and round the earth the Great Turtle traveled, never stopping, not even for a moment's rest.

"One day, as the Great Turtle was passing through the African grassland, one knee buckled beneath him. Two floppy-eared elephants fell off his back. 'Look what I've done,' cried the Great Turtle. I'll have to leave you behind.'

"'Don't worry, Great Turtle,' said the elephants. 'We're happy here in the grassland. And why don't you also leave our friends the lions and giraffes? They would like it here too.'

"'Very well,' said the Great Turtle, tilting to one side. The lions and giraffes rolled off his back. So did the ostriches, hyenas, zebras, warthogs, and gazelles. 'Have a nice time,' said the Great Turtle. 'I'll miss you.' Then the Great Turtle continued to walk the earth, feeling just a bit lighter than before."

Yessa stopped to rest. She looked around and saw she
had been joined by two tapirs, a pair of jaguars, a couple of
hummingbirds, two anteaters, a sloth and her mate, two
parrots, and a pair of tamarin monkeys. Yessa looked up at
the sky and went on.

"Soon the Great Turtle arrived at the edge of the Arctic Ocean. Before he knew what was happening, he slipped on the ice, and the whales, sea otters, seals, and polar bears glided off his back into the icy sea.

"'Oh no,' cried the Great Turtle. 'Look how clumsy I have been!'

"But the whales and the others shouted back: 'We like the Arctic Ocean. We want to stay here forever.'

"'Very well,' the Great Turtle said, 'but I'll miss you.' Then the Great Turtle continued on his way around the world."

Yessa passed a pond. Two frogs, two fire salamanders, and a couple of chameleons followed along to hear Yessa's story. So did two soft-shelled turtles and a pair of whirligigs.

"The desert of the Middle East was dry and dusty," Yessa continued. "The Great Turtle was parched with thirst. Suddenly, just beyond the next sand dune, he saw a pool of fresh oasis water. The Great Turtle hurled himself toward the mirage, then stumbled and realized he had made a mistake. Camels, scorpions, vultures, and cobras slipped off the Great Turtle's back, landing in the hot desert.

"'Oh no,' cried the Great Turtle. 'Look how foolish I have been!' But the camels, cobras, and others called back, 'Don't worry, Great Turtle. We want to make our home here in the desert.'

"'Very well,' said the Great Turtle, 'but I'll miss you.' Then the Great Turtle left the desert in search of a cool drink and crisp mountain air."

Fruit bats, orangutans, rhinos, peacocks,
pandas, and birds of paradise—two of every kind—
came to hear Yessa's story.

"High in the Himalayas, the source of the Ganges River, the Great Turtle quenched his thirst.

"There he left behind the yaks, the snow leopards, and the ibexes.

"In Australia, the Great Turtle watched the sunset. By the light of the twinkling stars, he found a home for the koala bears, the kangaroos, the kookaburras and the dingoes.

"And in the South American rain forest, the anacondas, the crocodiles, and the capybaras saw the Amazon River and bid the Great Turtle farewell."

Storm clouds gathered as the animals followed along, listening to Yessa's story, on their way to Yessa's brother's place.

"At last, after finding a home for every animal he had carried on his back, the Great Turtle was free to rest. But where, he wondered, would he like to make *his* home?

"'I'm at home in the desert,' said the Great Turtle. 'I'm at home in the forest. I'm at home in the grasslands, the marshes, and the sea. I could live almost anywhere, except for the air. But where would I most like to be?'

"For a long, long time, the Great Turtle could not make up his mind. Finally, he decided, 'I have seen all there is to see in the world, and I think I would most like to live on an island.'

"And so, when the world was still very new, the Great Turtle finally came to the Galápagos, or Turtle Islands. There he lived happily with the cormorants and herons and scarlet-colored crabs, and the seabirds called boobies. And there the Great Turtle rested."

A cold wind was blowing from every direction by the time Yessa had finished her story. The afternoon sky was as dark as night. The animals huddled together while Yessa knocked on her brother's door.

"Hello, Sister Yessa!" said her brother. "Welcome!"
Then Brother Noah swung wide the doors to his ark. Yessa
ushered in all the animals, two by two. Together, they closed
the doors to the ark just as the rain began to fall.

It rained for a long, long time. And the rest? Well ... that's another story.